Saving Shadows

Graphic Prose Poetry and Micro-lit

Saving Shadows

Graphic Prose Poetry and Micro-lit

Eugen Bacon

Illustrated by
Elena Betti

NEWCON PRESS

NewCon Press
England

First edition, published in the UK December 2021
by NewCon Press

NCP 267 (hardback)
NCP 268 (softback)

10 9 8 7 6 5 4 3 2 1

ISBN:
(hardback) 978-1-914953-04-0
(softback) 978-1-914953-05-7

Cover image and internal illustrations by Elena Betti, all original to this collection.
Back cover layout by Ian Whates

Minor editorial meddling by Ian Whates
Interior layout by Ian Whates and Eugen Bacon

Contents

Dedication

Bottom line is…
   She knows
      To Genni

      For indulging an enchantment of
      Language and metaphor
        To Ian Whates

        For getting, really getting
        My longing and seethe
          To Elena Betti

          For a winking river
          You're my delta
            To Dominique Hecq

Eugen Bacon

The Non-introduction

This collection of dark speculative micro-lit is a within-without response, an inner-outer gasp. The fiction recollects the dystopian nature of our today world: the covid-19 pandemic, the murder of George Floyd in 8 minutes 46 seconds, a symbol of police brutality.

Black lives matter.
The US presidential elections
The world watching
Everything unsettled
Text is an anchor
Actuality in the uncanny.
I gaze at a thunder-lit vista.
  Crashing.
    Roaring.
      It's no speculation.

Eugen Bacon

Unfinished

Survival reduced to pickets wakes me at night. Walls painted in stench, each day the beginning of my last. A siren of coppers chases rioters waving placards about paradigm shifts. Faces of my dead friends break out from the wind, imprint on each uniform's head, sketching shapes with colourless lips. Hearts weeping, bones humming. I exit by an alleyway, words raining like a president's bisque full of grime. I duck into cold roads of the city, walls pissing unfinished graffiti: I. Can't. Brea... A hobo with an umbrella hands me a parcel of dreams. More sirens – is there a better life? I take each folded dream and its prosthetic limbs, flick it to immortality. Text is your legacy! I call to the drifter losing himself in the brolly as I flee. Eat it! Lest the world murmurs oaths buried in your manuscript.

Unfinished

In a café

In a Café...

by the rampage, all the chairs are carved in limestone
because granite and alabaster cost too much.
Attendants are picked for lasting – more than
sandstone sounds just right. They float on teargas
without coughing, but their skins are full of burning.
Clientele are the ghosts of Mau Mau, John Lennon
and Pussy Riot. It's not the likes of these that sashay
with guards or inmates in the know, but they walk on
water. Today's talk is on the meander of time in a 6
by 8, steel or brick walled, no angling for parole as
you flirt with quarter worms slipping off stale crusts.
There's a depth beneath each brow, eyes full of
whispers that float in clouds above activists with soft
bodies falling like feathers. But the crowd is a
meniscus, fully cushioned and evened out, unyielding
to a line of police officers swallowed in masks. I see
oceans, la-di-da, a shimmer of hope in a new
yesterday, but today's a long way to the sea. I'm a
blind fish without a name and, right now, I can't
breathe.

Eugen Bacon

Caught on Camera

i've been searching for menus
that worry you out of cooking
cream flour whipped crème fraiche broiled
into a roux of nonstop impulse and lack of air
it's a promise of no immunity
restless ghosts scraped from generations
of colour with hardcore spatulas and marinated ignorance
disconnect the pot from the stove and you foray into willow
patterns of lethal force caught on camera
a litter of roadkill on an ivory table that's unsettling to watch
with its mismatched leftovers of no respect no dignity.

Caught on camera

Eugen Bacon

Happiness

Happiness…

in the months ahead is like a certificate of competence framed on the wall

embossed with a signature no insight to the toil that its owner has endured better than most hard to keep a lid on it when joy flees without a chorus

leaving behind an evanescence of ghosts and shared memories full of guidelines

on how to supervise misplaced glee

making vows is no more than a wee boy deadly as a firearm taking up the tale.

Eugen Bacon

The Ghost of a Graph

at the cusp of human and animal what brings you by is something
tragic
or a coincidence of strangehood /
you're poised with a needle whose tip is moist with a conspiracy
etched in numbers
and people are dying /
it takes time from initial moments to new scrutiny for officers of
the sovereign state
to act in the interest of the vulnerable or their actions to reach
global fuss /
researchers responding to data as part of a study
on the scatter of streetlamps and ethnic disparity
sequin stories of calamity and gore
    but are powerless
    to trend replicas
    on body cams
    clicking across a
    bridge to quietus
    in an inferno
    of contempt.

The ghost of a graph

Fifty metre penalty

Fifty-Metre Penalty

Because of her skill with the ball, people asked if she had extra
toes. She fell into three tackles, the clock now ticking. The field
normally hummed: now it was empty save for crowd photos. She
was bigger than the Beatles. Lots of minutes in those legs. A
nudge off the side of her boot: the footie whistled in deadtime
through the posts. Truth is she never took them for granted, her
time with them always in forward. Each kick was a metaphor
surrounding a husband's head. Spoils of war – she'd been married
thrice. Taught her well to read the ball. Nothing wide. No
mutations. That's what people didn't understand. Her hunger was
as there as a ghost. Connecting through a cool change, always,
always, hit the scoreboard.

Eugen Bacon

It's a Doofus

Escape is a burst of tears stowed with an eon. Next [*n.* /nɛkst] is temporality. Held in abeyance at a wonky intersection of slog and poise. An interchange of fact and fiction. Imagine this: a cerebral download metamorphosed with a nincompoop. The world is spinning with lost chronicles, missing ballots, sad songs. A jaunt of storms. A zigzag of lightning. Crackling to stillness at the foot of a brand new gravestone.

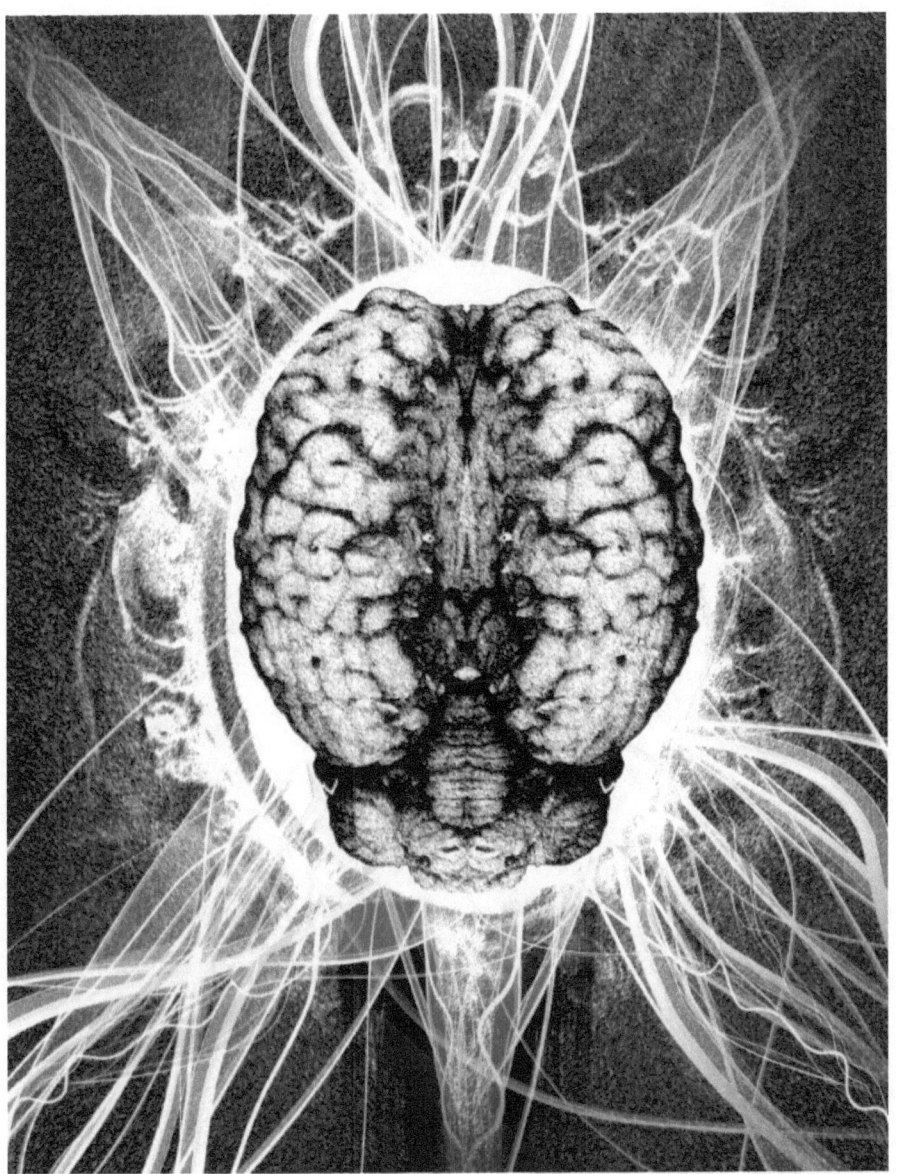

It's a doofus

Emergency services are sleeping

Emergency Services Are Sleeping

The popular tabloid ran a column on rampant variants spreading
at a Human Nature concert in a small-town bookstore. Be brave
it's a new Cold War, says a sufficient voice, unmasked by the
wails of tail-up kittens facing singing mirrors wearing white
gloves. Metaphor is unavoidable but allowed with corrective
lenses,
    trumpets and quarantine
    in a growing list
    of exposure sites
    now at capacity.

Eugen Bacon

A Costly Legacy

authority is total the way it's gotta be
  black lives matter   cofveve   how about bleach
    a bad grouping of tornadoes   cast doubt on facts
      about what imperilled   the world's agenda
    how fraud paled   the troika laundromat
  and what's with   turkey's gas for gold
a new variant of virus?

the dirt   scandals   a hand overplayed
  violent   deadly   incompatible with law
    arrogance   racism   antifa done it
      senators forsook   a scene of crime
    shaking heads at   find some votes
  everyone there   saw what happened
the world not there   gasped it happened.

bonnie and clyde   make this go away
  is it constitutional   who's fake news
    but nobody's asking   where the ventilators
      it's pinocchio's nose   dead right it is
    a plan is close   let's go back to the regular
  but a question for scholars   is it just politics
a vote is all it takes   or a secret pardon.

a mist blanket

she walks with a gap across a city choked in smoke   each day
disrupted as cynics protest pundits joke   theories fly about the
cavernous hole in her torso   why tar-shined ravens and deathwatch beetles soar through it   no one offers a mist blanket so
she can fold her wings at midnight   she looks at herself
mutters a prayer or a dream of rings
gives anyone who looks   an opus of her hollow

Eugen Bacon

This is Rain

when gods spewed their ire /*n. never indifference*/
  on floodlit citizens
    rain fell as certificates on the faithful
    but not all felt the storm
    just those beamed by searchlight

      awed by the phenomenon of *untouched*
      the unrained huddled in rainbows
        quizzed who was next sodden
          they stared at each other   reflections   held from speaking
          clouds billowed   swallowed waters   concluded their onus

        only then was it clear   the illuminati were gone
          first bleached   then gulped
            lifetimes washed   one by one as mud ribbons
            pasts unspaced
              quagmires expunged
              in a torrent of rain

This is rain

Saving shadows

Saving Shadows

What words keep you all there in an age of bias: appellations of choice, memory, sabre or epiphany? Perhaps an audio book of chimp paradigms for when you're bloomin' wretched. Lock the cask from shadows and darkness. Never want priests, fairies, politicians, sentries, trappers or paramours.

Become an ode.

Be water.

The Deep State

You can't cure the number of deaths by tossing reason into a vanishing spell that whisks the value of testing and puffs into a dusk of protesting.

- Unmarked vans detain humans as zoos re-open.

- Hackers steal vaccines camouflaged as mushy peas, broccoli and asparagus, shaping the taste away from children. It's an assertion of presence that tweaks the Darwinian theory of evolution: no variation, inheritance, selection or time.

- In winter's freeze the devil's nose is outside a mask freed from a myth where djinns and gargoyles hurl curses from every world into this broken one.

- What you can't cure is a lack of purpose that ticks to unending time.

The deep state

Blurred

Blurred

this quiet dawn you ring 000 and get a spray of kisses through
your phone /
you turn on the radio callers are suitors wooing you by name /
you think this fate is stolen   take your sedan for a car wash /
garage people blow your interior windows with red petals say
you are customer of the year extra protective wax dash console
clay treatment on da house /
you wonder what you remember what happened when and if
later you'll sit alone on a stool sipping brandy shoving a bowl of
bar nut mix down your throat /
as your bodies tangle and the mixologist says you're not
impervious you understand the world is not as you made it /
all that happened was a hoax
and this here is real

Psst!

Want one of these?

1. She's Lady Million, ochre and gold. Real memory, real history, she smells of a beautiful century.

2. What's her past? Ebony wood. Sex and lime. Untameable script, percussive word after word. She's the ghost of a finger, ta-pa-tap-tap. The door to a touchscreen juggling vowels and promises.

3. Ta-pitty-tap. A museum de luxe, devilish immorality. Silent in shelved dreams catalogued first by urgency, then mutation.

4. Ta-pa-tap-tap. Ta-pitty-tap. Long after your roar, she's left for the circus of messiahs whose tents are empty yet filled with reds, moors and hunkering.

Psst!

A voice in monotone

A Voice in Monotone...

will tell you about spikes in elective surgery to resuscitate dying
professions / where to find the best portions of idiocy in elected
officials / when to cancel your sanity insurance, how to hack
what's behind the precipitous number of infections /
what's best as a guide for panic buying
that's when you find the scrawl of a note to self /
scratched on a wall
notwithstanding the bloodshed a crossover novel will take you to
supreme calm.

Dégustation

takes my legs out when i dream of *un caffè* awash with cocktail
lights   swollen with black patrons encircled by neat-clad waiters
chimes of cutlery soft buzzing of chit chat   i savour a rib-eye
bathed in natural jus   nip from a bordeaux glass rich red with
bold tannins of syrah straight from tuscany   what about that
covid put it on the boot
a bender with the left foot just outside penalty
got the job done in the first quarter of an age of uncertainty
through to the siren that never wails

Dégustation

It's a boggle

It's A Boggle

On one side of letters, we pursue sound but trip on dialect: Is it
zed or zee? Etch or heytch? Look at you or yoo, how sum full
[*stuff some fool*] made sure a buffalo might well be a kaffalo or
a boof. And try insiGHt on a riotous mob! If 'a unique' is a
wooden-faced motley, it's a loss to contend with person-driven
letters and wooing to flirt with AI: machine learning and data
driven perception. Let's talk about smart cities and super
machines. Shapeshifting freeways, a metropolis of the future.
Multi-directional rush hours, self-adjusting bodies.
If we strung tomorrow into a new specimen of letters that
pushed its own boundaries, it'd be a pluri-dimensional
geometry of colour, sound, shimmer, lick, touch, dream and
sixth sense. Costumed with no proclamation or exegesis, just
vowelled with ankles and silk. Conjunctioned with lips and
fingers to manifest all days ahead. It'll become an intergalactic
typeshift. And overnight planets will scrabble and dance. Make
words with foes.
Even a pandemic will have no answers.

Too Little

You walked five years back, two years forth confined in a
bungalow until your soles wrote epigraphs on the wailing carpet.
You stubbed crescents and boulevards into old cities facing a
pantry but felt plateaus of shift when a postie buzzed your door.
You emerged shaggy-toed, braise-minded with 1,825 dawns
whose nonfiction overlooked to connect thoroughfares of alone
viewpoints in what turned out to be mere months. It was an
existence that tabloids adored, stamped with tenacious
commentary – the sort that trundles in the makings of antiquity.
But naught won a Pulitzer.

Destination

the place that reminds you of home has deserts and seas

they scorch or hump in scars and pleas

you drag your heart through heavens and earths

in endless quests to find holy burghs

now and then to a sex shop   crematorium

but what you see are memories   pandemonium

nothing white or laurel   just closed roads   aspirin

and a frigging /*frɪgɪŋ adj. rude, emphasis*/ migraine

slinking nowhere near home

full of turbulence and foam

wired and ravenous for   rib eye

its cancelled visa tells of a new strain   begging whiskey

Million-Dollar Deficit

Mercurial, not moody, he says. Whistling, taking flight, rustling sweet wrappers – like this he's basically twelve. Laughing at his own farts. He spreads on your skin, a filter of sun ray through street corners. You disremember unpredictable rain. He purrs, a kitten on your chest. You forget the cat that spits. The kettle that hisses. The librarian all sour. Ice cubes wetting your pillow. You can't remember why he's here. No safety upgrade plan. Just an instant asset write-off. Together in lockdown.

Million-dollar deficit

No crowds in the stadium

No Crowds in the Stadium

An orgy of tangled lies is savage bait not as deadly as the flu.
Novel or viral, each untruth bears symbolic weight before going
sober as a scrolling ticker in the news. Vitamins and painkillers,
steroids that expose flaws. Broken windows in a vale of shadows.
Sons and daughters hoist newfangled coffins. Right now. By the
hundreds. Of thousands. No breakthrough to solving this case of
hazard lights flashing. Bells tolling in a maze of crisis. Residual
with the loss of taste. Where's cartoon brilliance in a year like
this? Faces on billboards of decades past. Memory does not
escape a whole lot more. Lie still—it's not entirely a virtual event.
Are you the one dead? Always best
to pick up the phone.

Ornaments for Sale

Fifty bucks a week: confidence to spend again. A burden is the kingmaker that crowns a shopping calendar. Thirty percent off ditching the office. Cash bonus with hands-free door openers. A portable dishwasher for fifty-pack ultraviolet masks.
Wearable air filters – ornaments on sale.
It's your chance to save yourself.
Disinfect the future. Today the wind is dusty. Light rain through the night.
No extra charge.

Ornaments for sale

Strategizing on cobwebs

Strategizing on Cobwebs

The Committee investigating the Commission found consensus
that rules were broken when you forced People into a Bubble. It's
a cosmic crime, said the Minister of Think Big and Small Things
Happen. He was a feathered swoop with a sunburnt crest;
interchangeable friends with the Minister of Budget Cuts:
a token bird watcher – any quill would do.
The Minister of This Scene Out of Your Mind was sacred about
boneyards.
He connected with deals that huddled over take-out coffee,
gravestones where deadhearts clawed out
to put coffers into your pockets. The Minister of Tastes Even
Better When Someone Else is Cooking found scapegoats for
underperforming pension during a pandemic.
Roasted them Pendle-witch style until the phone rang or more
soulless arrived.

Eugen Bacon

A Breaking News Alert

… dons a rainbow mask and livestream freedom of anonymity
and projection
the mask locks in metaphors of emotions
angst and confusion above all rage
because it's rubbish to scramble behind locked windows
screening ideology from crows and ravens
what violation is there when arcades of chaos are full of extinct
animals
and fragments of spells that animate new creatures /
once upon a time quarantine meant something
until taboos went horribly wrong in local colour /
unseen clashes never aired after midnight
posturing as criticism or the absence of story
is the detritus of folklore inciting incidents
in a presidential speech on stolen ground /
now we wait.

A breaking news alert

Eugen Bacon

If you step off toilet paper

If You Step Off Toilet Paper...

and into a hosting arrangement, you must make sure there's enough data and no fake walls stuck under your feet. It's no small disaster. Try opening the advice box on top of the chiffonier – it will dispatch an approval workflow for new poems into a cautious world, epics daily columned on bleak futures.

Ace, ice, heat, fragile. Solid

Ace

is not an Uber you step into, step out of to recover from a weekend of decadence on your way to a shit office.

Ice

is not a retreat from a pandemic, even Wall Street is not immune.

Heat

is yesterday when you didn't think welfare payment was a thing.

Fragile

is a rare look at a radical author whose text hums, taut in its dialogue.

Solid

is the secret you unlock of corruption and grief, an ashy-haired novelist, face all seasoned, cloaking the collapse of a marriage with unseasonable weather. Observing as a poet a fire menace that coughs its flames to leave the world burning, burning.

Ace, ice, heat, fragile. Solid

What's belief?

What's Belief...

But memories, tides, longings
Finders keepers: what's lost, who's noticed.

A python shimmers under floodlights in the
Empty grandstands at Gate F of the stadium.

Oblivious to tubular steel, concrete piers, light towers
Convinced of invisibility, forgetting earthly forms of a night-time
game
Its bulbous head sways side to side.

Coned- and rodded-pupils in a fixated gaze at curses, epiphanies,
rhetoric
Slinking from forked tongues and the synthetics of the dark web
on lit outdoors
Disembodied voices – the peril never over – where's the feeblest
link, and how Ambiguous to trust? There's no four-minute
warning.

Eugen Bacon

His Love

'BUG HUG,' he said, an endearment that goes either way. 'It's a
stinger, nothing bent. Be alright.'

She studied the whiplash on her cheek, the momentum/
choreography of his fingers from her jaw to the eyebrow. Felt
extraordinary for yanking from his core blackthorn, not sloe
plum/silvered flowers.

Her flaw got her decked. 'Put an eye on it,' he said. 'Lid on the
lip too.'

She wrapped the bub in a pram – that was autumns ago.

Now she considers with fragility and in slow motion the
merits of those moments. His constructed narrative gathering
unexpectedness from her discordant recollection to sudden
lucidity unobscured by a false bottom.

News on vaccines, guns, family violence, polls, polies and
policing break the unseen sentence of a real story pirouetting in a
fever dream inside her head.

She lays peonies on her daughter's tomb. And the terrible
secret of a horned beast that sailed through the middle

Of love and disdain.

His love

It's a Trident

If accidents happen on the job the devil's in the detail, running,
smelling weird, Gasping, 'Bitch, make it count.' Ephesians: hell's
inside Earth. Physics: hell's Bollocks. Antigravity's not hot or
cold – 444.6 degrees Celsius' just about.
When brimstone turns to gasoline, the lake of fire lights.
Refuse your coins, fold your arms at the collection.
Use your alms to pay down the mortgage.
Why stoke unicorns and determinism,
Judgement below the earth.
It's a foraged apple,
The jury's wrong,
Maybe right.
But always
Acting
Free.

Sweepless

Darkness disperses into a hallelujah of Andromeda and The Milky Way.

It's a new anthem of sand – there it is, and still ardent your broom.

You throw water and dreams at it, now it's an oasis bedded on silt.

Pregnant with stars over the universe and your heart.

You can watch it all night, see what happens.

It spirals and bulges from the epicentre.

You watch it all day as you sweep.

Shape codewords in your mind.

But you fall asleep smiling.

A broom in your hand.

Tons of Liquid Oxygen Buckle Too Late Under Strain

Bones crumble, molecules, energy. It'll be weird at first, the next
ten years. The carnage of a decade – it's the work of us in a
rasping burr. Devouring the universe as we'd contest sausages.
Disaster capitalism is a thing. Unscientific thinking promotes
yoga, acupuncture, myotherapy to purge a pandemic. The Health
Ministry is missing in action. When the rich do nothing, the poor
perish. Bitcoin wipes nostalgia clean. Billowing in the clouds: the
face of a vulture fully beaked/talons on alert. A formation of
birds oblivious in a C down below. The ICU is a deathcamp.
Tents! More tents! Unconscious in a rickshaw. Tickets on the
black market bury gone flesh. A gasp for oxygen. Plumes. A
dance of flames some days we try to forget. Pretending we're
tourists hardened in the last sun, but our hearts are shattered in
hotspots and clusters as grief visits. Pyres burn. 3689 body bags
in a single day. Underreported in a second, third wave. The scale
of a crisis, one nation burns.
Meanwhile conspiracists mushroom dumb shit about
reengineered sex.
Going viral: Satan's microchips.

Tons of liquid oxygen buckle too late under strain

Where to next

Where to Next?

It's a process of plaque that can lead to gingivitis.
From symptoms to diagnosis: what's a good equation for the
arcane?
A lipstick-stained toothbrush focused on a white lie. An optic-
white streetlight – removes stains of dark rye toast with wild
berry jam from the mouth of a fruit loop.
A deep cream cleanser – it has menthol, sodium hydroxide (not
hydroxychloroquine), potassium cetyl phosphate, no concentrate, no
preservatives.
Just a bullshit detector that records faces,
makes them bob like balloons falling out of dreams.
The task force director is getting exasperated, writhing in the
dark.
Treble death in the last three days – can the head of homicide
solve this?
The virus will 'go away' says a dumb leader, confident he's raising
Lazarus.

Eugen Bacon

Long-Term Consequences

It's an incompleteness theory based on anti-prosody.
We're at war with an imbecile wheezing sewers of losses
Dragging a mire of conspiracy halfwits.
Loose-lipped polies who should know better
Act in an alternate universe like they don't.
The world needs a vaccine for scattered chaos
Every twenty seconds in a lame duck era.
Seagulls whistle allegations that lack a legal tactic.
It's a dead letter that keeps citizens entertained/on guard.
An interactive virus that's a social whore
Strikes with fangs every ten minutes.
Only too neatly until further notice
Outside the perimeter of said halfwits.

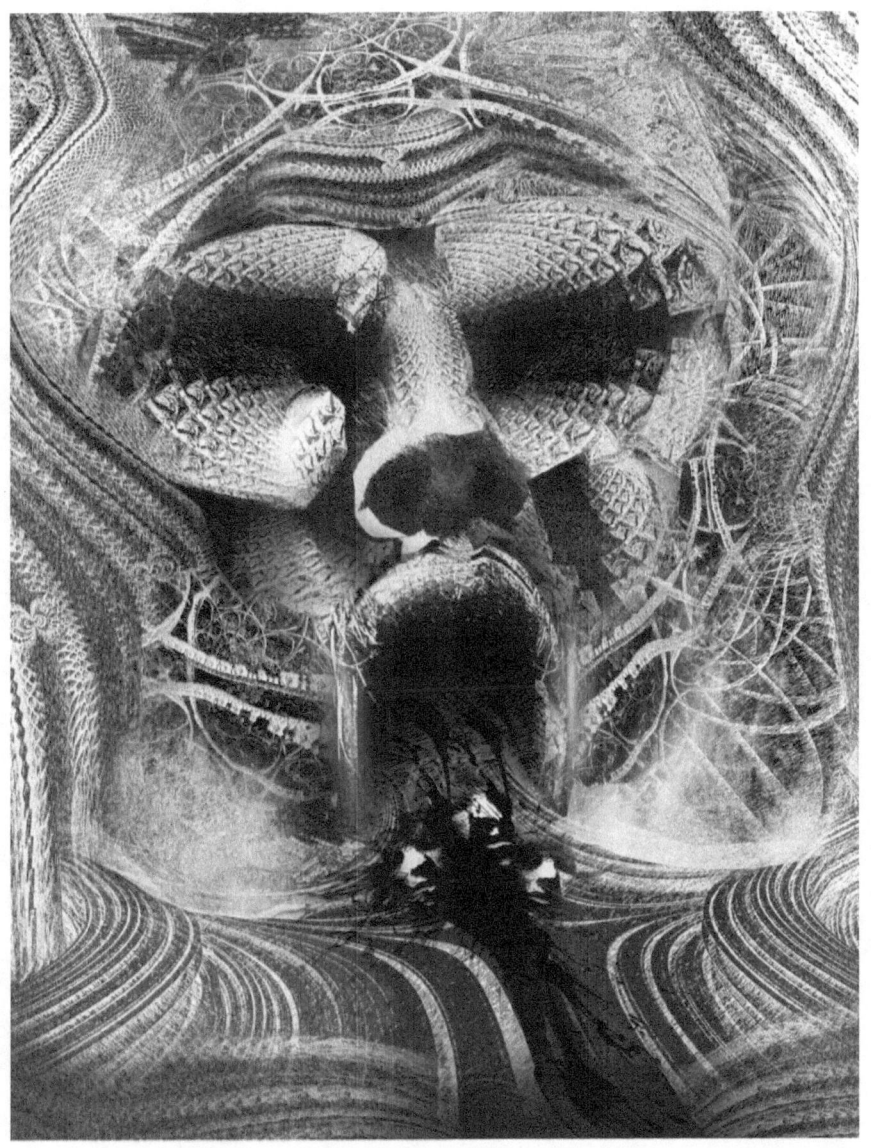

Long-term consequences

Misbelief

Misbelief

In a city of umbrellas and trees, people were generally pleasant.

Conversation fringed on deserts, famine but mostly diffusion.

Tourists left in wonderment at libraries filled with jungle, pelting rain.

Outside was bone-dry. Scorching afternoons tranquil

As watercolours unlicked by downpour.

We stumbled on an assassination of a bible in broad daylight.

Then it was a dictionary that knew too much.

Justice slithered towards a textbook, then another.

The book riot was all gently done.

Eugen Bacon

Innovators

We inherited dread and disremembered the liberty of babes sat
carefree on naked grass, curious fingers touching rainbow leaf
beetles that can never be pets.
We broke our daughters from strangers, dabbed at tiny palms
with fluids that
Assured us with *Added Aloe Vera, 70% Alcohol, Kills 99.99% of
Germs.*
Our new game, Rub-Your-Hands-Together, covered all surfaces
But it got into their eyes and their mouths, and they wailed.
We tutored them about masks and lockdowns,
Not bouncy winds and countryside photos.
We assembled words to tell about death
About death aboutdeathdeathdeath
What language speaks of life?

She Knows

Bottom line is… frog music is ribbit grunt hoot but why through the night from a pond or a creek in a sweet serenade that keeps her awake yet sleeps the baby and him / she breathes in closes her nostrils pushes out through her lips so she can ribbit grunt hoot but only whistles peeps clucks a stone's throw to the moss in his heart

Bottom line is… once it was easy like a boat into a jetty / holding hands was never against the rip / now she sits alone on sand and pebbles waiting for wash to pull her offshore / she's on the lip of an edgy current / the water's lick at eight feet per second

Bottom line is… she drowns again again / her life flashes in multi choice she (a) gulps to go back! to three yards of marriage   an epoch of waste (b) tries not to panic (c) finds the dignity of a storm (d) survival-floats to all of the above

Bottom line is… she moon-hauls to no webbed ecstasy just sirens wailing F# in 8th octave then a high C / she's on dry land legs spread wearing odd socks   her toes hurt for a long time / doesn't take a genius on comas / near-death / daemons to say don't worry love   cough yourself quiet   take a deep breath and go just go to whatever the fuck you things do

Bottom line is... second sight picks her colours of the day / rosy skirt dusky blouse / she knows which shoes open-toed no stockings waits for the 3rd lift / an itch on her palm's money on the way / the tic on her eyelid's bad news setting sail / black iron enters her gut someone she knows dies

Bottom line is... she sees the sex of an unborn child but is polite even when a spectre is sat on your shoulder   more so when a broken ghost has lost its address / she blinks at the mirror's unrepentant gaze because second sight
is a bitch / she knows

Bottom line is... she   knows

Plots Gathered Under the Eaves

the cloud is a sea of rain   tears in black waters that don't dissolve
206 bones 32 teeth   it's a day of no blood   just blot and rot on
which rove beetles/bottle flies can be anything but
conjunctions/interjections he explored without the retro of an ice
pick   no aria of a blade   just lost time understanding
buoyancy   how an object is equal to its weight in displaced
water sie pushed against gravity   kicked and gulped as he
listened to the semantics of   hir exclamations until sie lost squeal
then sight he calmed sie in lexicon   words in greek and arabic on
what happens in the throes of dying   how hearing and touch are
the last senses to go when hir brain shuts down   now sie floats
like a gas inflated orb or a balloon hir putrefaction is more a noun
than a pronoun less a preposition than an adverb/across the road
is a billboard for a closing-down sale   sie floats condemned
in sentences curled around the meaning of hir body   he watches
the ethereal adjectives of hir indigo feet as they float in a notion
of memory vanished in mist   once sie was his betelgeuse   the
supernova when it happened shattered with an alibi of unbuttered
toast   his hands crystalled into white sand and a hoodoo of deja-
vu   plots gathered under eaves one tottering sunday

Eugen Bacon

It's Less About Life

If ghosts need certitude their lights are dim coming home.
You keep them at bay, sometimes you become one.
Why did you die?
A day of deliberation turns a city into a fortress.
A drift of the accordion warms for more to come.
A song about fingernails ploughing out of graves.
They're a bit out of whack, *yadidida.*
Too many questions. *Yadi. Yadi. Yadi.*
The cat creeps into a bin, *yadidida.*
Losses on all sides. *Yadi. Yadi. Yadi.*
Sea salt on whiskers. A whiff of 'melly sardines.
Piths of departed apples.
Stare out of habit.
Then ask in abstract language.
About free will, inoculation.
Save your gaze for missing boaties, oxymorons. Jaws.
Crumped-up sequins, smiles that slip. Make rules as you go.
Stay out late, feel the words. *Yadidida.*
Clues and a clock full of doomsday bring you home.
Entitled innocents – is missing forever? *Yadi. Yadi. Yadi.*
She wears a knot of ribbons shedding paradoxes in the sand.
Her pocket's full of uneasy, tourism no-good news.
Bells toll: I'll be gone. Why did you die?

on a scale of howls

when we leave   we carry chiffoniers   cramped
  with gods of deception   guile   encamped
    with sprites   who make us hostage   from what matters
    we sow   souls from ashore   as case numbers shatter
   yet again   amid a surge of dying warriors   attacking plagues
we weigh   each life   by worth of our demagogues
 atop   beacon towers   ball-roomed in malice
lips out   twiddling chaos   paralysis
dirges   undulating   ripples
we trudge   souls crippled
as the fiddle   on a scale of howls
in 1-10   feeds new ghouls.

Eugen Bacon

Blessings, or Banishments

a cracked harmonium chimes

for the unbroken journal

with a tale of trees

that sit in an office

demand unforged sheets

to cancel culture on deforestation /

we get a chainsaw but saturday

knocks with rain

nodding leaves all sodden wet /

the next tree lurks in our heads

like a wedding or a fiend's crotch

or an unwelcome confessional

as dreadful as a chapel hymn /

the last tree stomps with sixth sense

fog-wearing eyes

a snarl of ravens

a skit in slapstick

about deathwatch played solo

with hints   ink-black words

scattered all wrong

Blessings, or banishments

She was too sick to have a cat

She Was Too Sick to Have A Cat

… but a mesmer-eyed kitty made a statement from the sill. Its
unblinking stare spoke in almond shapes, told of a bus trip along
the Great Ocean Road,
past a grotto and a loch, some redwoods and the mariner, an
hour at the lookout. Black bamboos lined the shore.
Bug-faced fish with beating hearts leapt to break the surface but
she couldn't catch them. She opened the window, dry-coughed
not to overcommit. But the cat gave a
slow-eyed blink hosting galaxies and sprang full of purr to her
ankles.
It snuggled in her onesie, its snores stretched forever in a paradise
where there was no fever, joint pain, moroseness or lack of
breathing.
Just a vacuum to cool her burning and
for a moment she could pass out.

Eugen Bacon

What the Mask Saw

the mask whirls before restrictions her string and feather wings
pirouette to a ditty
of human truths engorged with antibodies flouting type-1 activity
she takes to incandescent skies gazes at the glimmer of a man
with naked feet buying roses snapdragons proteas delphiniums so
a florist can keep aloft ahead of lockdown five mouths to feed
a sign at the supermarket says elderly only   a neon at a vacant
mall
dusty with sunset rugs broadcasts quarantine bingo
free penguin parade on a virtual bridge

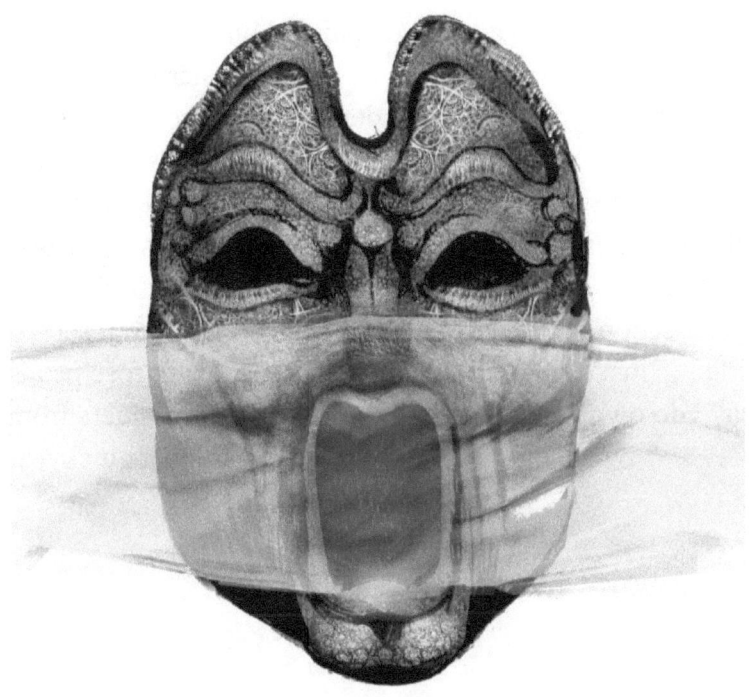

What the mask saw

the mask hip-hops to opera livestreaming a sonorous eloquence
of the cello
a silvery melancholy of the flute a solemn transcendence of the
oboe a rippling wave
in loops of the violin playing Dante all the way to paradise on the
other side

#

the mask perceives a post box painted blue emblazoned in
white across his chest
saying thank you first responders   studies the corner shop
meting hand sanitisers to
a food bank   discerns clapping   the city's applause for carers
lauds to hearten ventilators tubes monitors pumps in a frost-
white icu   she trembles with a bride in an off-shoulder
mermaid-scoop whose groom has no aisle runner no reserved
seating   just a ring pillow unity candle and silk rose petals
they say i do on a zoom wedding thronged with strangers from
the cork of the universe in a quickyear

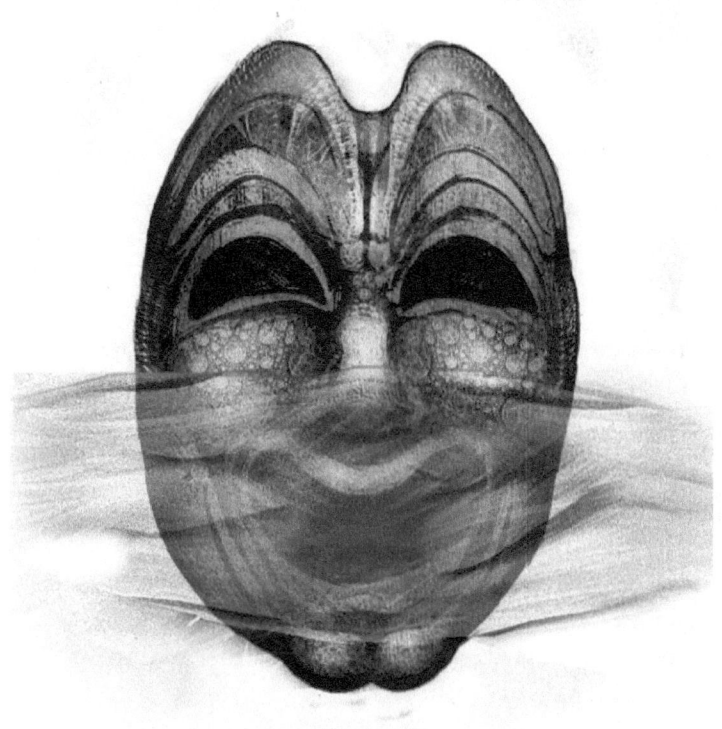

What the mask then saw

The mask sees hope is a realm shifting patients to ocean breaks
quintessential rainbows   concealed kindliness of strangers /
resilience is a diamond planet adorning love across its balconies
gladdening lakes in a pink shimmer of flamingos irradiating the
waters / future is the first day of school after eons of piano in iso
an amity of campaigners hooking elbows with coppers bending
knees
on newfound lands that closely resemble earth

Eugen Bacon

Frame of Reference

Love is…

an apartment   lit with hand-painted watercolours vases and
photographs
memories in a frame   a big screen right there   65-inch high
definition
you make a cuppa   vanilla chai   one minute in the microwave
milk's just right   now look at the bills

Love is…

a toilet seat   practical   engineered for a purpose works because
of gravity
it's not to eat breakfast / check your emails   just a healthy
disposal unit
takes what you discard   saves you from a megacolon
how long   can you go without

Love is…

a box of tissues   craving crumbs of sourdough   drools of soup
it's not a sofa that knows skin and bums   feet and cheeks
it's not a letter from the bank   a copy of your insurance
just a box of tissues   unremembered on a coffee table

Love is…

an uber   sometimes on time sometimes it isn't   you don't know
what you get
but you can cancel the fare   one driver asks do you want water
takes you to a destination   rates you out of five
you rate them back   is that what you want

Love is…

an airport   hosts in immaculate caps   here's your boarding pass
travel information   declarations   restrictions that apply
but all you think is hotspots   not the WI-FI kind
there's not enough runway

Love is…

a swimming pool   azure water ebony lines   sunlit rays through a
glassy roof
a bench you never sit on   a silent clock tick tock tick tocking as
you dive
mostly you're alone   bubbles as you breathe   shimmers on the
lanes
dead lizard on the floor   water's ruffled when you leave

Love is…

a poem   brimming fire and ocean   blizzard and air
it looks at you askance   you know better than to succumb   but
you do
as you float the universe in spaceless time   screening memory
feeling   filaments
of the lunar spirit   unable to wrestle hallucination   a twilight of
foreboding that never leaves

Eugen Bacon

An Earnest Blackness

There's an animal tacked in my hair, and it hangs like a mirror I
can't see.
It's full of silence, shadows, asking are we caged, or free?
Sometimes
It licks my skin but doesn't disturb me. When I reach up to touch
it,
I can't remember where it is, if it is. Perhaps it's more cunning
Than I thought, hiding its pawprints. Patiently waiting to
Catch me with reflections of ebony nights, white stars,
Burnt-orange dust. I know and I don't, the hum of
Rain on a tin roof. The taste of my grandma's
Sweetened mangoes – moulded like
A donkey's ear plucked fresh from
A tree that's a silhouette above
My mother's bones.

An earnest blackness

Eugen Bacon

Nuance no longer exists

Nuance No Longer Exists

You carry evaluation forms this time of the year just weeks to
winter solstice when daytime is shortest, and rain is falling to
awaken fingers itching with big questions hidden inside cucumber
dumplings, metaphors and bins. Strangers climb into secure
spaces, and drafts in progress embolden home-grown radicals. A
sticky date liberation no longer does it, and you remember stories
out of perfection. It's no comfort that there's no passport and
you're the voice of the narrator's spectre profiling
innovation/disconnection yet nudging the reader to reply with
masking birthed from truth/illusion. A cluster spreads across
households, growing infections into an outbreak alive to
possibility of genomic sequencing after you replace all
gravestones. But, of course, you can't.
Or won't.

Eugen Bacon

Unprecedented

The wandering cow like a serial ghoul was desperate but defiant.
She added daffodils and rainbows to each masterpiece and it
travelled unchewed to the rumen and then to the reticulum.
Satiated from the eating, she rested and waited and thought. She
calculated the right time to cough up bits of cud, now chewing
them completely before she swallowed. It
raced through her gut, exploded from her bovine ass and
splashed pat in a polychromatic mess on the polished shoe of a
visiting president just checking in on his way to the next
apocalypse with a new detail – they had all mastered the perfect
low ponytail, and those who hadn't wore tail-hair wigs.
As cameras flashed, the cow took back to her eating and
continued to be an artist ruminating how to dung the next
political dunderhead.

Echoes on Dream Windows

Your body's flamboyant with tonight's headlines.
An unruly bugaboo peers through the sight: X marks the spot.

It bobs through the city, in, out, back, on the freeway.
It's coming for you: the ghost of your harming... glaring in half-
light.

It crawls through malls. Stadiums. Superstores.
The pulse of the bogey one's radiance attuned to your core.

Don't linger one minute, it's a mutant, this gremlin.
Nemesis. Kismet... Naming doesn't matter... seen anything like it?

Your spectre is coming, all jiggly for your corpse.
A dead march in a porous poem 'til a new morrow is nigh.

Also by Eugen Bacon

Fiction

Claiming T-Mo

Her Bitch Dress

It's Folking Political

Hadithi & The State of Black Speculative Fiction (with Milton Davis)

Black Moon: Graphic Speculative Flash Fiction

The Road to Woop Woop & Other Stories

Ivory's Story

Speculate (with Dominique Hecq)

Danged Black Thing

Mage of Fools [forthcoming, March 2022]

Non-Fiction

Writing Speculative Fiction

About the Creator

Eugen Bacon is African Australian, a computer scientist mentally re-engineered into creative writing. Her novella *Ivory's Story* was shortlisted in the 2020 British Science Fiction Association Awards. Her work has won, been shortlisted, longlisted or commended in national and international awards, including the Foreword Book of the Year Awards, Bridport Prize, Copyright Agency Prize, Australian Shadows Awards, Ditmar Awards and Nommo Awards for Speculative Fiction by Africans. Recent works: *Danged Black Thing*, a short story collection by Transit Lounge Publishing (2021) and *Mage of Fools*, an Afrofuturistic dystopian novel by Meerkat Press (2022).

Website: eugenbacon.com Twitter: @EugenBacon

About the Illustrator

Elena Betti is an experienced illustrator whose works have been published worldwide. Driven by her deep love for art and imagination, she can envision the concepts requested by her clients and provide a reliable service for professional customers. Find her here:

illustratumsite.wordpress.com.

Also from NewCon Press

Burning Brightly edited by Ian Whates
Celebrating 50 years of Novacon, featuring a mix of original fiction and first time reprints of stories written by former Guests of Honour, including **Iain M. Banks, Peter F. Hamilton, Stephen Baxter, Justina Robson, Paul McAuley, Jaine Fenn, Adrian Tchaikovsky, Anne Nicholls, Geoff Ryman, Ian R. MacLeod, Juliet E. McKenna,** and more…

Just Three Words – V.C. Linde
Dazzling poetry from an award winning poet, each poem inspired by three words donated by authors or celebrities, including **Mark Gatiss, Alan Moore, China Miéville, Tanith Lee, Iain M. Banks, Charlaine Harris, Kelley Armstrong, Ramsey Campbell, Trudi Canavan, Pat Cadigan, Guy Gavriel Kay, Lauren Beukes, Brent Weeks, Jeff VanderMeer** and many more.

Ivory's Story – Eugen Bacon
In the streets of Sydney a killer stalks the night, slaughtering innocents. The victims seem unconnected, yet Investigating Officer Ivory Tembo is convinced the killings are far from random. The case soon leads Ivory into places she never imagined. In order to stop the killings and save the life of the man she loves, she must reach deep into her past, uncover secrets of her heritage, break a demon's curse, and somehow unify two worlds.

Dark Harvest – Cat Sparks
Award-winning author Cat Sparks writes science fiction with a distinct Australian flavour – stories steeped in the desperate anarchy of Mad Max futures, redolent with scorching sun and the harshness of desert sands, but her narratives reach deeper than that. In her tales of ordinary people adapting to post-apocalyptic futures, she casts a light on what it means to be human; the good and the bad, the noble and the shameful.